Poetic Philosophy Presents

Narrative Translations Designed for Accessibility

Plato's *Laws* (Books I & II)

The Puppet, the Lawgiver, and the War Within

By Plato

Translated by Jason Kassel, PhD

© 2025

Recursive Publishing

Table of Contents

Plato's Laws: Book I

624a-625b: Law by God or Man?

Athenian: Strangers, were your laws authored by a God, or man?

Cleinias: Stranger, a God. In truth, a God. Among us Cretans, he is said to have been Zeus. In Lacedaemon, where our friend here comes from, I believe they say that Apollo is their lawgiver. Wouldn't they, Megillus?

Megillus: Certainly.

Athenian: Do you believe Homer who says that Minos was inspired to make laws for your cities after conversing with his father Zeus every ninth year?

Cleinias: Yes, that is our tradition. And there was his brother Rhadamanthus, who is reputed to have been the most just of all men. We Cretans believe he administered justice righteously while alive and earned his reputation.

Athenian: Yes, a noble reputation that's worthy of a son of Zeus. As you and Megillus have been trained in these institutions, will you be willing to give me an account of your government and laws? We are walking, and can pass the time pleasantly while talking about them. I am told that the distance from Cnosus to the cave and temple of Zeus is considerable. Doubtless there are shady places under the lofty trees, which will protect us from this scorching sun. Being no longer young, we may often stop to rest beneath them, and get over the whole journey without difficulty, beguiling the time by conversation.

625c-626b: Institutions of War

CLEINIAS: Stranger, if we proceed onward we shall come to that large and beautiful cypress grove. We may repose and converse in the green meadows.

ATHENIAN: Very good.

CLEINIAS: Very good, indeed. It will be even better when we see them. Let's move on cheerily.

ATHENIAN: I am willing. Tell me why the Spartan law ordained common meals, gymnastic exercises, and the wearing of arms.

CLEINIAS: Stranger, I think that our institutions are easily intelligible. Look at the character of our country. In Thessaly, they have horsemen because it is large and flat. In Crete, the ground in our country is unequal and more adapted to running. If you have runners, you must have light arms because you can't carry a heavy weight while running, and bows and arrows are convenient and light. All of these regulations have been made with a view towards war. It appears to me that the legislator looked to war in all his arrangements. If I am not mistaken, he instituted common meals for a similar reason. He saw that citizens in the field are naturally compelled to take their meals together for the sake of mutual protection. To me, he seems to have thought the world foolish for not understanding that men are always at war with one another. During war, persons are regularly appointed to protect armies and common meals occur regularly. This should continue in peace because, he would say, what men term peace is only a name. In reality, every city is in a natural state of war with every other. This is everlasting and isn't proclaimed by heralds. If you look closely, you'll find that the Cretan legislator intended all institutions, private as well as public, to be arranged with a view toward war. In doing so, he was under the impression that the person defeated in battle doesn't have valuable possessions or institutions because the conquerors have acquired all of their good things.

626c-626e: States Focused on War

Athenian: Can you be more explicit about the Cretan government's principle? You seem to imagine that a well-governed state ought to be ordered so as to conquer all other states in war. Am I right in supposing this to be your meaning?

Cleinias: Certainly. If I am not mistaken, our Lacedaemonian friend will agree with me.

Megillus: How could any Lacedaemonian say anything else?

Athenian: Does this apply to villages as well as states?

Cleinias: To both alike.

Athenian: The same?

Cleinias: Yes.

Athenian: And the village will have the same war of house against house, and individual against individual?

Cleinias: The same.

Athenian: Then should we say that each man should conceive himself to be his own enemy?

Cleinias: O, Athenian stranger. I won't call you an inhabitant of Attica, for you should be named after the goddess herself. You go back to first principles, and have thrown a light upon the argument. I am now better able to understand what I was just saying. All men are publicly one another's enemies, and each man privately is his own enemy.

Athenian: My good sir, what do you mean?

Cleinias: There is always victory and defeat. A man has his best victory, and his worst defeat against himself, not at the hands of another. This shows that, within every one of us, there is a war against ourselves going on.

626e-627c: The Central Unifying Principle

Athenian: Let us reverse the argument's order. Starting with every individual being either his own superior or inferior, does the same principle hold for the house, village, and state?

Cleinias: Do you mean that each has its own principle of superiority or inferiority?

Athenian: Yes.

Cleinias: You're right to ask the question. There certainly is such a principle, and above all in states. The state whose better citizens won victory over the mob, and the inferior classes, may be said to be better than itself (self-superior) and justly praised for gaining such a victory, or censured for being defeated.

Athenian: Whether the worst ever really conquers the best is a question which requires more discussion, and let's leave it for the present. However, I understand your meaning to be that citizens of the same race, who live in the same cities, may unjustly conspire and, having superiority in numbers, may overcome and enslave the few who are just. When these unjust citizens prevail, the state may be truly called inferior and therefore bad. When their superiors defeat them, it is therefore good.

Cleinias: Stranger, your remark is a paradox we can't deny.

627c-628a: The Three Judges

ATHENIAN: Here is another case to consider. One man and woman can create a family with several brothers. Most likely, the majority may be unjust, and only a few will be just.

CLEINIAS: Very possibly.

ATHENIAN: Should we properly call this family and household superior when the just brothers conquer their unjust brethren, and inferior when they are conquered? We aren't considering what may or may not be proper or customary, only the natural principles of right and wrong in laws.

CLEINIAS: Stranger, what you say is most true.

MEGILLUS: In my opinion, quite excellent so far.

ATHENIAN: Does a judge exist over these brethren?

CLEINIAS: Certainly.

ATHENIAN: Who is a better judge for determining whether men should govern themselves? Is it the man who destroyed the bad and appointed the good? Or the man who allowed the bad to live so long if they voluntarily submitted to being governed by the good? I suppose a third judge to weigh the scale of excellence might find that the family was distracted, and didn't destroy anyone. Instead, he reconciled the family and gave them laws which they mutually observed. In this way, he was able to keep them friends.

CLEINIAS: The last would be by far the best sort of judge and legislator.

628a-628c: The Lawgiver's Desire: No Civil War

ATHENIAN: The aim of all the laws given by the combination of judge and legislator would be the reverse of war.

CLEINIAS: Very true.

ATHENIAN: What about he who constitutes the state and orders the life of man? Does he focus on external war or the kind of intestinal war called civil? After all, no one wants civil war in his own state and, when it does occur, everyone wishes it to end as soon as possible.

CLEINIAS: He should be focused on preventing civil war.

ATHENIAN: Would he prefer civil war to end with one party being destroyed, and the other completely victorious? Or, would he prefer that peace, friendship, and reconciliation be re-established so that they can attend to foreign enemies?

CLEINIAS: In the case of his own state, everyone would desire the latter.

ATHENIAN: Wouldn't that also be the legislator's desire?

CLEINIAS: Certainly.

ATHENIAN: Wouldn't everyone want to make laws for the sake of the best?

CLEINIAS: To be sure.

628c-628e: The State is Unhealthy

ATHENIAN: War, whether foreign or civil, is not good and needs to be deprecated. It is best to have peace and goodwill. The state's victory over itself isn't merely a good thing, it is absolutely necessary. A man might as well say the sick body purged by medicine is in the best state while forgetting the body shouldn't need to be purged. Likewise, the true statesman who aims for the happiness of the individual or state, doesn't look primarily towards external war. The sound legislator orders the state for peace to prepare for war, he doesn't order the state for war to create peace.

CLEINIAS: Stranger, this remark of yours seems true. However, unless I am mistaken, neither our or the

Lacedaemonian's institutions are entirely aimed at preparing for war.

628e-629d: Warrior Poet: Tyrtaeus

ATHENIAN: Let's not rudely quarrel about your legislators. Seeing that we and they are equally in earnest, let's gently question them. Please follow my argument closely: I call your attention to Tyrtaeus who was born in Athens, but became a Spartan citizen. More than any man, he was eager for war. He said, "I sing not, I care not, about any man, even the richest man who possesses every good (and then he lists them), if he is always a brave warrior." I imagine you must have heard his poems. Our Lacedaemonian friend has probably heard more than enough of them.

MEGILLUS: Very true.

CLEINIAS: They have found their way from Lacedaemon to Crete.

ATHENIAN: Let us ask Tyrtaeus together: We will say to him, O most inspired, wise, and good poet, the excellent praise you bestowed on those who excel in war proves that you are wise and good. Megillus, Cleinias of Cnosus, and I agree with you entirely. However, are we sure we're speaking of the same man? Tell us, do you agree that there are two kinds of war? What would you say? A far inferior man to Tyrtaeus would have no difficulty in replying truthfully that there are two kinds of war. One is universally called civil war and, as we agreed, is the worst of all wars. We should all admit that having a falling out with nations of a different race is a far milder form of warfare.

CLEINIAS: Certainly, far milder.

629d-630b: Warrior Poet: Theognis

ATHENIAN: Which type of war do you praise and blame in high-flown strains? If I judge from your words, I suppose you speak of foreign war when you say that you abominate those 'Who refuse to look upon fields of blood, and not draw near and strike at their enemies.' We shall naturally say: Tyrtaeus, it seems you praise those who distinguish themselves in external and foreign war. He must admit this.

CLEINIAS: Evidently.

ATHENIAN: They are good, but the better men display virtue in the greatest of all battles. We also have a poet as witness. His name is Theognis, who was a citizen of Megara in Sicily. He says, 'Cyrnus, a man faithful in civil broil is worth their weight in gold and silver.' We affirm that this man faces a more difficult kind of war, and that he is far better than the other man. The difference is similar to justice, temperance, and wisdom when united with courage. All four are better than courage alone. In civil strife, a man can't be faithful and good because he lacks every virtue. Tyrtaeus praises mercenary soldiers willing to stand at post and be ready to die. Yet, these men are, almost without exception, insolent, unjust, and violent men. Truly the most senseless of human beings. What is my point?

630b-630d: Perfect Justice

Athenian: Like any divine legislator worthy of consideration, Apollo established Crete above all others because he made laws with the greatest virtue in mind. According to Theognis, that is loyalty in the hour of danger. Truly, this may be called perfect justice. Whereas, Tyrtaeus gives high praise to a virtue that is good enough for the moment. However, among the virtues, courage is in fourth place for dignity (i.e., it ranks after justice, temperance, and wisdom.).

CLEINIAS: Stranger, we are degrading our inspired lawgiver to a rank which is far beneath him.

630d-631b: The Aim of a Lawgiver

ATHENIAN: I think that we degrade ourselves by imagining that Lycurgus and Minos created laws in Lacedaemon and Crete with a view toward war.

CLEINIAS: Then, what should we say?

ATHENIAN: Unless I'm mistaken, when speaking on behalf of a divine hero we must speak of truth and justice. The legislator we speak of made laws with a view towards all of virtue, not merely a part of virtue, and not the lowest virtue. All of virtue. He devised classes of laws for different kinds of virtue but not in the way that modern inventors of laws make classes of law. Moderns only investigate and offer laws when they feel a need. One man's class of laws focuses on allotments and heiresses, another about assaults, and still others about ten thousand matters. We maintain that the right way of examining laws is to proceed as we have now done. I admired the spirit of your exposition and believe you were right to begin by saying virtue was the lawgiver's aim. I thought that you were wrong because you only viewed legislating through the least virtue (courage) and that led me to make my remarks. Will you allow me to explain how I should have liked to have heard you expound the matter?

CLEINIAS: By all means.

631b-631d: Divine vs Human Goods

ATHENIAN: Stranger, you ought to have said: With good reason, the Cretan laws are famous among the Hellenes. The object of laws is to make those who use them happy and Crete's laws confer every sort of good. There are two kinds of goods. One is human and the other divine. The human hangs upon the divine. The state which acquires the divine, simultaneously acquires the human. However, if it lacks the divine, it may not acquire either. Among human goods, health is first, beauty second, strength (i.e. swiftness in running and bodily agility) comes third, and wealth comes last. Not the blind God who promises wealth, but a God of keen sight who has wisdom as a companion. Wisdom is the chief leader of the divine class of goods, and then temperance. Together, wisdom and temperance form a union which, when combined with courage, leads to justice. The lowest virtue on the scale is courage. Naturally, all of these take precedence over human goods. This is the order the legislator must place them, and afterwards he will look to the divine when creating other ordinances for the citizens. The human looks up to the divine, and the divine looks to the leader's mind.

631d-632c: Lawgiver: Responsibilities

Athenian: Some of the lawgiver's ordinances will relate to marriage, procreation, and children's education (male and female). The lawgiver's duty is to take charge of his citizens throughout their lives from when they are young through old age. He is to punish and reward how they engage in intercourse with one another, and should consider their pains, pleasures, desires, and the strength of their passions. He should watch over them, and use the laws as his mouth to blame or praise them. Regarding perturbations of the soul arising out of anger, terror, misfortune, deliverance of prosperity, and other experiences that come to men through disease, war, poverty, or the opposite of all these. In all these states, the lawgiver should determine and teach good and evil. After this, the legislator should carefully manage how the citizens make money, and how it is spent. He should watch voluntarily and involuntarily contracts, and how they form and dissolve. He should see the order of all this, and consider whether their dealings with one another are just or unjust. Until civil life is ended, the lawgiver should honor those who obey the law, and impose fixed penalties on those who disobey. Finally, at the end, the lawgiver should consider funeral rites and ways in which the dead can be honored.

632c-632d: Law: Guardians

Athenian: Reviewing his work, the lawgiver will appoint guardians of the law to preside over his work. The intelligent will walk toward this, others will once there is true opinion, and then Mind will bind the ordinances together and show them to be in harmony with temperance and justice rather than wealth or ambition. Strangers, this is the spirit in which I was and am desirous that you should pursue the subject. I want to know the nature of all these things, and how they are arranged in the, they are termed, 'laws of Zeus,' and Minos and Lycurgus' Pythian Apollo. Although the order of law is far from being self-evident to the rest of mankind, let's use the experienced eyes of men trained by study or habit.

632d-632e: Goal: Model of Virtue as a Whole

CLEINIAS: Stranger, how shall we proceed?

ATHENIAN: We must begin again as before. First, let's consider the habit of courage and then discuss another virtue, and then another. In this way, we'll form a model of virtue as a whole. We'll use similar discourses to beguile ourselves along the way. By the grace of God, when we have gone through all the virtues, we'll show that the institutions I speak about look to virtue.

633a-633d: Virtue: Courage

MEGILLUS: Begin by criticizing Cleinias, the laws of Crete, and their praise of Zeus.

ATHENIAN: I will try to criticize you, me, as well as the person who praises Zeus. The argument focuses on a common concern. Tell me, didn't your legislator invent the common meals and then the gymnasia with a view toward war?[1]

MEGILLUS: Yes.

ATHENIAN: And what comes third, and fourth? I think we should enumerate the remaining parts of virtue

---

[1] The συσσίτιον (syssitia) were Spartan and Cretan common meals for men and youths.

in this way. We can call them parts or anything else provided the meaning is clear.

MEGILLUS: I and any other Lacedaemonian would reply that hunting is third.

ATHENIAN: Can you think what comes fourth and fifth?

MEGILLUS: I think that I can get as far as the fourth part. We Spartans endure pain in hand-to-hand fights or when we get a good beating for stealing.[2] For the Crypteia, or secret service, our people show endurance while wandering over the whole country day and night. Even in winter, they have to attend to themselves without a shoe on their foot or beds to lie on. In the violent summer heat, our citizens show marvelous endurance while exercising naked.[3] I could speak of an endless number of similar practices.

---

[2] This was training for boys which overlapped with ritual activity at the Sanctuary of Artemis Orthia, where they were made to steal from the altar under threat of being beaten if they were caught.

[3] The Gymnopaedia was an annual festival celebrated exclusively in ancient Sparta, and helped to define Spartan identity. It featured generations of naked Spartan men participating in war dancing and choral singing, with a large emphasis placed on age and generational groups.

ATHENIAN: O Lacedaemonian Stranger, this is excellent. How should we define courage? Does courage only combat fears and pains? Or, does it also combat desires, pleasures, and flatteries?   Isn't the power pleasure so tremendous that it can make respectable citizens' hearts melt like wax?

MEGILLUS: I should say the latter.

633d-634d: Institutions: Courage

ATHENIAN: You'll remember that our Cnosian friend had earlier spoken of a man or a city being inferior to themselves.[4] Weren't you, Cleinias?

CLEINIAS: I was.

ATHENIAN: My question is: Is the man overcome by pleasure truly inferior than the man overcome by pain?

CLEINIAS: I would say all men say it is more disgraceful to be overcome by pleasure and the man who is able to overcome pain is superior.

---

[4] 627a

ATHENIAN: Surely Apollo and Zeus did not create laws so that Sparta and Crete would have citizens with a one lame one-legged courage that was only capable of meeting painful attacks from the left, but impotent against insidious flattery from the right?

CLEINIAS: I would think not.

ATHENIAN: Then let me ask once more. What institutions do your states have so that citizens can equally brave endure pleasure and pain? To learn endurance, a person must be compelled through reward or induced. Is there a similar ordinance about pleasure? Tell me, do you have something of this nature? How do you regulate your citizens so they become brave against both pleasure and pain, conquering what they ought to conquer, and superior to their closest and most dangerous enemies?

MEGILLUS: Stranger, while I was able to tell you about many laws directed against pain, I don't know that I can point to a great or obvious example of similar institutions concerning pleasure. However, I might be able to mention some lesser provisions.

CLEINIAS: Cretan laws don't have anything equally prominent regarding pleasures as they do pain .

634c-634d: Old Men Talking Around the Young

ATHENIAN: My dear friends, it is very likely that, as we search for the true and good, we may have to censure one another's laws. In this event, we must take kindly to what another says, and not be offended.

CLEINIAS: Athenian Stranger, you are quite right, and we will do as you say.

ATHENIAN: Cleinias, at our time of life, we shouldn't feel irritation.

CLEINIAS: Certainly not.

ATHENIAN: At present, I won't determine whether it is right or wrong to censure Cretan or Lacedaemonian polities. However, I believe that I understand better than either of you what people say. Assuming your laws are reasonably good, they will contain a law forbidding young men to inquire which laws are right or wrong.

With one mouth and one voice the young must agree that the laws are all good and that they came from God. If someone says the contrary, he shouldn't be listened to. However, an old man who discusses defects in your laws may observe and communicate to a ruler or, when no young man is present, to an equal in years.

CLEINIAS: Stranger, you are like a diviner. Although you weren't present when laws were made, you seem to me to say what is true and have hit upon the legislator's meaning.

ATHENIAN: And now, as there are no young men present, and the legislator has given old men free license to speak and we are alone, we can discuss these matters properly.

CLEINIAS: True. Therefore, be as free as you like in your censure of our laws. There isn't any discredit to knowing what is wrong, and the person who generously receives what is said in a friendly spirit will be improved.

634d-635e: Becoming a Slave

Athenian: I am not going to say anything against your laws until I have examined them. However, I will raise doubts. Whether Greek or barbarian, you are the only people we know to whom the legislator gave commands regarding abstaining from great pleasures and amusements. Regarding pain and fear, the legislator determined that people who, from infancy onward, avoided pains, fears, and sorrows would run away when compelled to face foes who had been hardened. They wanted to avoid them becoming someone else's slaves.[5] Now, the legislator ought to have considered whether this was equally true of pleasure. He should have said to himself: From their youth upward, our citizens will be acquainted with the greatest of pleasures so that they may be able endure the temptations of pleasure. Without being disciplined to refrain from all things evil, they will never be able to overcome the sweet feeling of

---

[5] This section is important because the Athenian Stranger is recommending institutions to endure pleasure so that citizens will avoid slavery, but his political philosophy paradoxically relies on enslavement through absolute obedience.

pleasure. It will be worse than if they couldn't endure pain. They will become slaves to the worst of mankind: those who endure pleasures. One half of the citizen's soul will become a slave, while the other half will remain free. However, they won't be worthy of truly being called, in the true sense, men and freemen. Tell me whether you assent to my words?

Cleinias: On first hearing, what you say appears to be the truth. But it would be childish and simple if we hastily came to a conclusion about such important matters.

635e-636e: Pleasure and Pain

Athenian: Suppose we consider the virtue of temperance. What Cretan or Lacedaemon institutions are like your military institutions but relate to temperance? Are any of them different from those of any ordinary state?

Megillus: That is not an easy question to answer. I would say the common meals and gymnastic exercises have been excellently devised for promoting both temperance and courage.

Athenian: Stranger, it seems to be difficult to make words and facts coincide when talking about a state without there being a dispute about meaning. As in the human body, a regimen which does one type of good simultaneously does a type of harm. We can't say that one course of treatment can be applied to each particular constitution. Your gymnasia and common meals do a great deal of good. However, as shown by the Milesian, Boeotian, and Thurian youth, they can also cause evil and civil troubles. In general, these institutions tend toward degrading the ancient and natural custom of love below the level of beasts. This is true of most other states which cultivate gymnastics. Whether in jest or serious, I think natural pleasure arises from sexual intercourse between men and women. It is contrary to nature to have sexual intercourse with the same sex. The bold attempt was due to their being enslaved to pleasure. Cretans justify unnatural pleasures by the story of lawgiving Zeus and his mortal lover Ganymede. Leaving the story aside, we may observe that when speculating about laws, for both states and individuals, the discourse revolves around pleasure and pain. These are nature's two flowing fountains, and the man who draws from them where, when, and as much as he ought to is happy. This holds for men, animals, and states. The man who indulges in them ignorantly, and at the wrong time, is unhappy.

636e-638a: Dionysiac Festivals

MEGILLUS: Stranger, I admit that your words are well spoken, and I don't know how to answer. Still, I think Sparta's lawgiver was right to forbid pleasure. I shall let Cleinias, my Cnosian friend, defend Cretan laws but, to me, Sparta has the best laws regarding pleasure in the world. In general, the law has driven out mankind's wildest pleasure, license, and folly, Sparta's country and towns are devoid of revelries and the incitements which accompany their pleasures. If someone meets a drunk and disorderly person, they immediately have him severely punished and won't let him off on any pretense. Not even during a Dionysiac festival as often happens during 'on the cart' performances.[6] I have seen an entire city of Tarentine colonists drunk at a Dionysiac festival. However, that doesn't happen among us.

ATHENIAN: O Lacedaemonian Stranger, these festivities are praiseworthy when there is a spirit of endurance. However, when they aren't regulated, they are senseless. In self-defense, an Athenian can point out the licentiousness which exists among your women.[7] However, whenever anyone accuses a Tarentine, Athenian, or you then there is always one answer that exonerates the practice from impropriety. After a stranger expresses wonder at what he sees, inhabitants naturally answer: O stranger, Wonder not. This is our custom, and you may have some other custom.

---

[6] The opening of the festival featured a procession to the Theater of Dionysus bearing a wooden statue of the god. As the first day progressed, choruses of men and boys representing the ten political tribes of Athens held dithyrambic competitions. The day concluded with the sacrifice of a bull and a communal feast. At the Feast of Dionysus in Athens it was customary for revelers mounted on wagons to indulge in scurrilous language during the processions.

[7] Here the Athenian Stranger is implicitly acknowledging that Athens engages in the festivals as described.

However, my friends, we are not speaking about men in general, but the merits and defects of lawgivers. Thus, let us discourse on an important subject that will seriously challenge the legislator's discrimination - intoxication. I am speaking of intoxication, not abstention from wine. Should we follow the custom of the Scythians, Persians, Carthaginians, Celts, Iberians, and Thracians? They are all warlike nations who engage in intoxication while your custom is to abstain. The Scythians and Thracians, both men and women, drink unmixed wine and pour it on their garments because, to them, it is a happy and glorious institution. The Persians have more moderation than the Thracians and Scythians, but they have other practices of luxury which you also reject.

Megillus: If we took up arms, Sparta could defeat all these nations.

638a-638b: Becoming Enslaved

Athenian: Yes, but there have been, and will always be, flights and pursuits which can't be explained.

In battle, victory or defeat doesn't prove whether institutions are good or bad. Larger states conquer and enslave states with fewer numbers, as the Syracusans have done to the Locrians (who appear to be the best-governed people in their part of the world) or as Athenians have done to the Ceans.[8] There are ten thousand other instances of the same sort of thing. Thus, this doesn't sufficiently get to the point. Instead of discussing victories and defeats, let's form a conclusion about each institution and simply say whether a custom is honorable or not. First, let me tell you how we will estimate good and bad.

Megillus: How?

638b-638e: Good and Bad

Athenian: A discussion proceeds the wrong way when a topic is praised or censured at a moment's notice. Let me give you an illustration: You may suppose a person is praising wheat. However, without inquiring into what wheat is, and questions surrounding

---

[8] **Again, become become enslaved because their states are defeated at war.**

its effect, use, and procedures then, when something goes wrong, another person will instantly blame wheat. That is what we are doing in this discussion. Once we mentioned intoxication, one side was ready to praise and the other to censure. This is absurd. Either side can bring forth witnesses and people who approve. Some men have witnesses who think they are authorities on intoxication and they attest that those who abstain successfully conquer. Others will say abstention leads them to be conquered. We dispute this, and won't be satisfied to continue discussing the remaining laws in the same way. I would like to speak in another way about intoxication, which I hold to be the right one. After all, if absolute numbers are the criterion for truth, there are multiple nations who dispute the customs in your two cities?

MEGILLUS: I shall gladly welcome any correct method of inquiry.

639a-639e: Censuring Goats

ATHENIAN: What do you think of this: Suppose a person praised owning goats and then someone saw the goats eating without a goatherd. Doing mischief, the man decided to censure a goat for not having a proper keeper. Would censuring the goat in this way lead to any sense or justice?

MEGILLUS: Certainly not.

ATHENIAN: If a captain is regularly sea-sick, should we consider him to be a good captain because he has knowledge? What do you say?

MEGILLUS: I say that he isn't a good captain because, even though he has nautical skill, he is liable to sea-sickness.

ATHENIAN: What would you say of the commander of an army? Will his military skill allow him to command if he's cowardly, sick, and drunk with fear when danger comes?

MEGILLUS: Impossible.

ATHENIAN: What if he's a coward without skill?

MEGILLUS: He's a miserable fellow, and fit to command old women no men.

ATHENIAN: And what would you say of someone who blames or praises any sort of meeting which is intended by nature to have a ruler, and is doing well enough when under his presidency? The critic has never seen an orderly feast and society meeting controlled by a good president, but always sees one without a ruler or with a bad one. Are observers of this class supposed to value their words of praise or blame regarding such meetings?

MEGILLUS: Certainly not. If they've never seen, or attended, a rightly ordered meeting.

ATHENIAN: Reflect. Aren't banqueters and banquets supposed to constitute a kind of meeting?

MEGILLUS: Of course.

ATHENIAN: And has anyone ever seen a rightly ordered convivial meeting? Of course, you two will answer that you have never seen them at all. In your country, they are not customary or lawful. I have come across them in many different places, and moreover I have made inquiries about them wherever I went. I say, never did I see or hear of one carried on altogether rightly. In some few particulars they might be right, but in general they were utterly wrong.

639e-640b: Need for a Leader

CLEINIAS: Stranger, what do you mean by this remark? Explain. As you say, we are inexperienced in such matters and we wouldn't know what was right or wrong in such social meetings if we encountered them.

ATHENIAN: Likely enough. Let me try to be your instructor. You would acknowledge that there ought to be a leader for all sorts of man's gatherings ?

CLEINIAS: Certainly.

ATHENIAN: Just now, we said that war required a brave man to be leader?

CLEINIAS: We did.

ATHENIAN: The brave man is less likely to be disturbed by fears than the cowardly?

CLEINIAS: That again is true.

640b-641a: Leadership Qualities

ATHENIAN: If it were possible to have a general who was absolutely fearless and imperturbable, shouldn't we appoint him?

CLEINIAS: Assuredly.

ATHENIAN: However, we are not speaking of a general to command an army during a time of war, but of one to regulate another sort of meeting. One which happens when friend meets friend in time of peace.

CLEINIAS: True.

ATHENIAN: That sort of meeting is apt to be loud when attended drunk.

CLEINIAS: Certainly. It is the reverse of quiet.

ATHENIAN: Then revelers and soldiers each require a ruler?

CLEINIAS: To be sure, more than most.

ATHENIAN: If possible, shouldn't we provide them with a quiet ruler?

CLEINIAS: Of course.

ATHENIAN: He should be a man who understands society. It will be his duty to preserve and increase friendly feelings among the company.

CLEINIAS: Very true.

ATHENIAN: When we choose a ruler to be our master of revels, he should be wise. If he's young, drunken, and not over-wise, then only good fortune will save him from doing evil.

CLEINIAS: Only through singular good fortune will he be saved.

ATHENIAN: Now, suppose such associations are framed in the best way possible in states and a person blames, perhaps correctly, the associations.[9] If he sees a practice, and places blame on it for being mismanaged, even though no one else sees it mismanaged, he shows that he is unaware of the mismanagement. Second, he shows that he is unaware that everything done in this way will turn out to be wrong. This is because the ruler isn't sober. Don't you see that a drunken pilot or a

---

[9] Is this Socrates?

drunken ruler of any sort will ruin a ship, chariot, army? In short, anything which he controls?

641a-641d: Particular vs General

CLEINIAS: Stranger, your last remark is very true. I see the advantage of armies having good leaders who will give followers victory in war. This is a very great advantage as are other things. However, I do not see a similar advantage for individuals or states properly managing a feast. I want you to tell me - what great good is brought about once this drinking ordinance is established?

ATHENIAN: We can't identify a great good that accrues to the state from the right training of a single youth or chorus. This is because, in any particular instance, we can't deny that the good is not very great. If the question is, what is education good for in general, the answer is that education makes good men, good men act nobly and, because they are good and noble, they conquer their enemies in battle.[10] Education gives

---

[10] Earlier he said strength and numbers conquer in battle.

victory, but victory sometimes makes one forget how he was educated. After victory in war, many grow insolent which engenders innumerable evils. Many victories have been, and will be, suicidal to the victors. Education is never suicidal.

CLEINIAS: My friend, you seem to imply that, when rightly ordered convivial meetings are an important element of education.

ATHENIAN: Certainly I do.

641d-642b: Prelude to Discourse on Drinking

CLEINIAS: Can you show us that what you've been saying is true?

ATHENIAN: Stranger, the Gods haven't given man the attribute of being absolutely sure of truth when matters concern many opinions. I shall be happy to tell you what I think, especially as we are now proposing to enter a discussion concerning laws and constitutions.

CLEINIAS: Stranger, we want to hear your opinion about the questions now being raised.

ATHENIAN: Very good. I will find a way to present my meaning, and you shall try to have the gift of understanding. First, let me make an apology. Among all the Hellenes, the Athenian citizen is reputed to be a great talker. Sparta is renowned for brevity, and the Cretans for wit. I am afraid of appearing to elicit a long discourse out of very small materials. Drinking may appear to be a slight matter. However, it is one that nature requires to be ordered correctly with a clear and satisfactory treatment of necessary musical principles. There is much to be said about music as a part of general education. What would you say to leaving these matters for the present, and passing on to some other question of law?

642b-643a: Praise for Athens

MEGILLUS: O Athenian Stranger, you may not know that our family is the proxenus of your state.[11] I imagine that all boys, from their earliest youth, feel

---

[11] A "proxenus" was a citizen of a city state in ancient Greece appointed by another state to have charge of its interests and the welfare of its citizens while in his state.

kindly towards the state from which they are told they are proxeni. This is their second country and this has certainly been my own feeling.[12] I can well remember how, during boyhood, when Lacedaemonians praised or blamed the Athenians, I was told: 'See, Megillus, how ill or how well,' as the case might be, 'your state has treated us.' I became warmly attached to Athens because I had to fight battles against your detractors when I heard you had been attacked. I always like to hear someone speak in the Athenian tongue. The common saying is quite true, a good Athenian is more than ordinarily good. He is the only man who is not manufactured but, by the divine inspiration of his own nature, is freely and genuinely good.[13] Therefore, be assured that I shall like to hear you say whatever you have to say.

CLEINIAS: Stranger, when you've heard me speak you boldly say what's in your thoughts. Let me remind you that Crete is united towards you. My family included the prophet Epimenides, and you must have

---

[12] Sparta - through the story of the lame schoolteacher - are now part of Athens.
[13] not by outward compulsion but by inner disposition

heard the story of how, in accordance with the Oracle's response, he came to Athens ten years before the Persian war to offer sacrifices which the God commanded. At that time, the Athenians dreaded the Persian invasion. Epimenides said that for ten years they would not come and, when they did come, they would suffer more evil than they inflicted, and leave without having accomplished their objectives. At that time, our forefathers formed ties of hospitality. Thus, my parents instilled in me an ancient friendship with Athens.

ATHENIAN: You seem ready to listen. I am ready to perform an almost impossible task. Yet, I make the attempt. As the discussion begins, let me define the nature and power of education. This is how we will argue and travel towards the God Dionysus.[14]

CLEINIAS: Let us proceed, if you please.

---

[14] Think about this in terms of Nietzsche.

643b-644b: Objective of Education

ATHENIAN: I'll tell you what my notions of education are. Will you consider whether they satisfy you?

CLEINIAS: Let's hear.

ATHENIAN: According to my view, to be good at anything, the person must practice that thing from his youth upwards in both sport and earnest. For example, the man who is going to be a good builder, should play at building children's houses. He who is to be a good husbandman, at tilling the ground. Those who care for the young and their education should provide them with tools to mimic the thing they will be good at. This will allow them to learn the knowledge before it's required for their art. For example, the future carpenter should learn to measure or apply the line while playing, and the future warrior should be amused by learning riding (or some other exercise). With the help of amusements, the teacher should endeavor to direct the children's inclinations and pleasures to their final aim in life. The most important part of education is training rightly in the nursery. While playing, the child's soul should be guided to love the excellence he will have to perfect when a man. Do you agree with me thus far?

CLEINIAS: Certainly.

ATHENIAN: Let's not make education something ambiguous or ill-defined. At present, when speaking praise or blame about the bringing-up of each person, we say one man is educated, and another uneducated, although the uneducated man may be well educated as a retail trader, captain of a ship or the like. We are not speaking of education in this narrower sense. Instead, we're speaking of the education in virtue from youth upwards which makes a man eagerly pursue, and teaches him the ideal perfection of citizenship regarding how to rightly rule and obey. This is the only education which, upon our view, deserves the name. The other is a sort of training or mere cleverness apart from intelligence and justice which aims at the acquisition of wealth or bodily strength. It is mean and illiberal, and is not worthy to be called education at all. But let us not quarrel with one another about a word. Has the proposition taken hold? To wit, those who are rightly educated generally become good men. Education mustn't be disparaged because it is the first and fairest thing that the best of men can ever have, and though liable to take a wrong direction, it is capable of being reformed. And every man has the great business of working on this reform while he lives.

CLEINIAS: Very true. We entirely agree with you.

644b-644d: Are We One?

ATHENIAN: We agreed before that good men are able to rule themselves, and bad men are not.

CLEINIAS: Yes.

ATHENIAN: Let me now proceed to make the subject more clear by an illustration.

CLEINIAS: Proceed.

ATHENIAN: Do we consider ourselves to be one?[15]

---

[15] οὐκοῦν ἕνα μὲν ἡμῶν ἕκαστον αὐτὸν τιθῶμεν; - Alternative: May we assume that each of us by himself is a single unit?

CLEINIAS: We do.

ATHENIAN: And each of us has two counselors in his bosom, both of which are foolish and antagonistic. We call the one pleasure, and the other pain.

CLEINIAS: Exactly.

ATHENIAN: Regarding opinions about the future, we have the name 'expectations.' The name 'fear' when we expect pain, and 'hope' when we expect pleasure. In addition, the reflection about their good or evil, when embodied in a decree by the state, is called law.[16]

CLEINIAS: I am hardly able to follow you. However, please proceed as if I were.

MEGILLUS: I also can't follow.

644d-645c: Puppets of the Gods

Athenian: Let us think of this. Aren't each of us living beings a puppet of the Gods?[17] They either

---

[16] that which precedes pain bears the special name of "fear," and that which precedes pleasure the special name of "confidence"; and in addition to all these there is "calculation," pronouncing which of them is good, which bad; and "calculation," when it has become the public decree of the State, is named "law."

[17] This is connected to Dionysus. In a myth related to the ancient Greek mystery cult of Orphism, the Titans used a collection of toys — a mirror, golden apples, knucklebones, dolls, and spinning toys (a kohnos, and a rhombos) — to divert infant Dionysus' attention from the powers which Zeus had granted him, and successfully lure him. After cutting Dionysus into small pieces, they boiled him and ate his flesh.

created us to be their playthings, or did so with a purpose. We don't know which. We do know that affections towards them are like cords and strings pulling us in different and opposite ways, and towards opposite actions. This is the difference between virtue and vice. According to the argument, every man ought to grasp one cord, pull, and never let go. This is the sacred and golden cord of reason. We call this the common law of the state. There are cords of hard iron, but this one is soft and golden. There are others. We ought to cooperate with the best, which is law. While reason is beautiful, gentle, and isn't violent, her rule must have ministers in order to help the golden principle vanquish the other principles.[18] The morality story

---

However, Athena saved his beating heart and sent it to Zeus. The father of the gods sewed it into his thigh, from which Dionysus was reborn. there are many descriptions of true puppet shows which certainly existed in Ancient Greece. In The Banquet (chap. 4, §55) Xenophon (5th to 4th centuries BCE) tells us that among the guests invited by Callias to this symposion, a showman from Syracuse demonstrated his "puppet" (neurospaston, neurospasta = moved by sinews or threads see [lier]Neuropasto[/lier]), but it is difficult to determine the exact nature of this figure. At least this text provides testimony of the presence of different types of entertainer, probably including puppeteers. In his allegory of the cave (The Republic, Book 7) Plato (4th century BCE), in order to illustrate his thoughts on the illusory nature of the senses, also refers to a "maker of marvels" and his "wonders" (tois thaumatopoiois "those who perform feats of skill, magicians", often interpreted as "puppet showmen").

[18] Republic?

about our being puppets will make the expression 'superior or inferior to a man's self' clearer. The individual, who pulls the puppet's strings in this matter, and attains reason, should live according to its rule. The city, receiving the same from some god or from a person who has knowledge of these things, should embody it in a law, to guide internal and external dealings. This will allow us to clearly distinguish virtue and vice. When they have become clearer, education and other institutions will become clearer in a similar manner. In particular, the question of convivial entertainment, which may seem to be a very trifling matter which I have taken a great many more words than were necessary.[19]

Cleinias: The theme may turn out to be worthy of a longer discourse.

645c-646a: The Drinking Puppet

ATHENIAN: Let us proceed with an inquiry which really bears on our present object.

CLEINIAS: Proceed.

---

[19] Nietzsche

ATHENIAN: Suppose that we give our puppet a drink. What will be its effect on him?

CLEINIAS: You ask that question with what in view?

ATHENIAN: Nothing yet, I am asking generally - When the puppet drinks, what sort of result is likely to follow? I will endeavor to explain my meaning more clearly. I am now asking - Does the drinking of wine heighten and increase pleasures, pains, passions, and loves?

CLEINIAS: Very greatly.

ATHENIAN: And are perception, memory, opinion, and prudence heightened and increased? Don't these qualities desert a man entirely if he becomes saturated with drink?

CLEINIAS: Yes, they entirely desert him.

ATHENIAN: Doesn't he return to his young childhood state of soul?

CLEINIAS: He does.

ATHENIAN: And at that time he has the least control over himself?

CLEINIAS: The least.

ATHENIAN: And isn't he in a most wretched plight?

CLEINIAS: Most wretched.

ATHENIAN: Then both an old man and a drunkard become a child for the second time?

CLEINIAS: Stranger, that's well said.

ATHENIAN: Can we prove that we should encourage drinking instead of doing all we can to avoid it?

CLEINIAS: You were saying that you're ready to maintain such a doctrine.

646b-646e: The Doctrine

ATHENIAN: I am ready to explain my doctrine that encourages drinking wine instead of abstaining completely, especially as I see that you both declare to be anxious to hear me.

CLEINIAS: To be sure we are, if only to hear the strange and paradoxical assertion that a man ought of his own accord to plunge into utter degradation.

ATHENIAN: Are you speaking of the soul?

CLEINIAS: Yes.

ATHENIAN: My friend, what do you say about the body? Aren't you surprised that a person, of his own accord, would bring deformity, leanness, ugliness, and decrepitude upon himself?

CLEINIAS: Certainly.

ATHENIAN: However, when a man goes to a doctor's shop on his own accord and takes medicine,[20] isn't he aware that quickly, and for many days afterwards, his body will be in a state in which he'd rather die than accept it as the permanent condition of his life? Aren't those who train in gymnasia, at first reduced to a state of weakness?[21]

CLEINIAS: Yes, all that is well known.

---

[20] dispensaries to drink medicines
[21] Medical political analogy focused on pharmacy

ATHENIAN: Yet, they go of their own accord for the sake of the subsequent benefit?

CLEINIAS: Very good.

ATHENIAN: Can we conceive that this is true for other practices in the same way?

CLEINIAS: Certainly.

ATHENIAN: The same for the pastime of drinking wine. That is, if we are right in supposing that the same good effect follows?

CLEINIAS: To be sure.

ATHENIAN: If such convivialities should turn out to have any advantage equal in importance to that of gymnastic, they are in their very nature, inasmuch as they have no accompaniment of pain, to be preferred to mere bodily exercise,.

CLEINIAS: True, but I don't think we shall be able to discover any such benefits.

646e-647d: Two Fears

ATHENIAN: We must endeavor to show that convivialities bring benefits. Let me begin by asking you a question: Don't we distinguish between two different kinds of fear?

CLEINIAS: What are they?

ATHENIAN: There is fear of an expected evil.

CLEINIAS: Yes.

ATHENIAN: And there is fear of an evil reputation. That is, we're afraid of doing or saying something dishonorable and will be shamed. We fear being thought of as evil.

CLEINIAS: Certainly.

ATHENIAN: I call these the two fears. The second - which brings shame - is the opposite of pain and fear (it also opposite the greatest and most numerous pleasures).[22]

CLEINIAS: Very true.

ATHENIAN: And doesn't the legislator, and everyone who is good for anything, honor this greatest fear and call it 'reverence' and the reverse is called

---

'insolence?' He always deems the latter to be a very great evil to both individuals and states.

CLEINIAS: True.

ATHENIAN: Doesn't this fear preserve us in many important ways? What gives victory and safety in war? There are two things - confidence before enemies and fear of disgrace before friends.[23]

CLEINIAS: There are.

ATHENIAN: Then each of us should be fearless and fearful. We have now determined why we should be both.

CLEINIAS: Certainly.

647c-647e: Training for Fear

ATHENIAN: When we want to make a person fearless, we should use the law to draw him up so he faces his fears.

CLEINIAS: Clearly.

ATHENIAN: And to make him fearful in the right way, shouldn't we introduce him to, and train him to

---

[23] Not the fear of becoming enslaved?

take up arms against, shameless pleasures so he can overcome them? Or, does this principle apply to courage only? Why should the man who would be perfect in valor have to fight against and overcome his own natural character? If he is unpracticed and inexperienced in such conflicts, he won't be half the man he might have been. Are we to suppose it's otherwise with temperance? Should we believe that the man who never fought and conquered pleasures, lusts, and shameless, unrighteous temptations in earnestness, play, word, deed, and act will still be perfectly temperate?

CLEINIAS: A most unlikely supposition.

647e-648e: Fear Potion

ATHENIAN: Suppose that some God had given man a fear-potion, so that the more a man drank the more he regarded himself a child of misfortune, and that he feared everything happening or about to happen to him. Until the most courageous of men utterly lost his presence of mind and only returned to himself after sleeping off the potion's influence.

CLEINIAS: Stranger, has such a potion ever really been known among men?

ATHENIAN: No, but wouldn't the legislator use a potion such as this to test courage? Might we not go and say to him: 'O legislator, whether legislating for the Cretan, or any other state, wouldn't you like to have a touchstone of the courage and cowardice of your citizens?'[24]

CLEINIAS: Every one of them will answer: 'I would.'

ATHENIAN: 'And wouldn't you rather have a touchstone without risk or great danger?'

CLEINIAS: Everyone would agree with that.

---

[24] Bury uses the word 'test.' However, in choosing the word 'touchstone,' Jowett chose to define βασανίζω as both verb and noun. The verb meant: 'to test, to investigate, to examine, and to put to the test.' As a noun, a touchstone was a tool that tested purity of gold, silver, and other precious metals. Based on earlier writings, it is reasonable to assume Plato wants readers to visualize the tool. In Gorgias, Plato writes: "If my soul had happened to be made of gold, don't you think I would have been delighted to find one of those stones with which they test gold, and it confirmed that my soul had been properly tended" (486d). In the Republic, Plato writes: "Testing them more carefully than men do gold in the fire, to see if the man remains immune to such witchcraft and preserve his composure throughout" (3.413e).

ATHENIAN: 'And to make use of the potion, wouldn't you lead them into imaginary terrors to prove to them that they were being influenced by fear? Wouldn't you compel, exhort, and admonish them to become fearless? You would honor them, but anyone who won't act as you command through persuasion will be dishonored in all respects. If he underwent the trial well and manfully, wouldn't you let him go unscathed? And, if he performed poorly, wouldn't you inflict punishment? Or, would you abstain from using the potion altogether even though you have no reason to do so?'

CLEINIAS: Stranger, he'd certainly use the potion.

ATHENIAN: Compared to what is now in use, this mode of testing and training would be wonderfully easy, and might be applied to a single person, a few or, indeed, any number. The man who gave himself the potion, and didn't share it may prefer to contend, out of shame of being seen by the eye of man before becoming perfect, with his fears in solitude. Or, trusting the force of his own nature and habits, and believing he had already been sufficiently disciplined, he won't hesitate to train himself so that he can be within the company of others and display his power in being able to conquer the potion's irresistible changes without his virtue falling into any great unseemliness. He was always himself, and left before arriving at the last cup. He properly feared that he, like all other men, might be overcome by the potion.

CLEINIAS: Stranger, in that last case, the man might show temperance.

649a-649b: Fearlessness Potion

Athenian: Let us return to our lawgiver and say: 'Man has never received from the Gods a potion that induces fear and he hasn't discovered one for himself. Witchcraft has no place on our board.[25] However, is there a potion which tests being overly bold and engaging in excessive and indiscreet boasting?'

---

[25] for quacks I count not of our company - this is also a medical reference

Cleinias: I suppose he will say, yes. That is, wine is a fear potion.

Athenian: When we discussed what the lawgiver needs, doesn't wine produce the very opposite? When a man drinks wine, he begins to be more pleased with himself. The more he drinks, the more he is filled full of brave hopes, and conceits of power. The string of his tongue is loosened and, fancying himself wise, he brims with lawlessness. He has no more fear or respect, and is ready to do or say anything.

Cleinias: I think that everyone will admit the truth of your description.

Megillus: Certainly.

649b-650b: Art of Politics

Athenian: Let us remember that there are two things which should be cultivated in the soul - the greatest courage, and the greatest fear.

Cleinias: Which you said to be characteristic of reverence, if I am not mistaken.

Athenian: Thank you for reminding me. As courage and fearlessness are habits trained amid fear, shouldn't the opposite qualities also be trained among their opposites?

Cleinias: That is probably the case.

Athenian: There are times and seasons at which we are more commonly valiant and bold by nature. On these occasions, we ought to train ourselves to be as free from impudence and shamelessness as possible, and to be afraid to say or suffer or do anything that is base.

Cleinias: True.

Athenian: Aren't we apt to be bold and shameless in moments when influenced by anger, love, pride, ignorance, avarice, cowardice? Or when maddened by the intoxicating workings of pleasure, wealth, beauty, strength? However, if care is taken in its use, the festive use of wine can test and train a man's character. Which is cheaper, more innocent, and less risky - working and making bargains with a morose, savage, and unjust man while alone? Or, while being companions at the festival of Dionysus? When a man is a slave to the pleasures of sex, isn't it a more dangerous test to entrust him with one's daughters, sons, and wife? Wouldn't this imperil one's own nearest and dearest, simply to discover the disposition of the man's soul? I might mention innumerable cases in which characters get to know one another through wine's playful method of inspection without paying dearly for the experience. I don't believe that a Cretan, or any man, will doubt that getting to know a man's soul through a playful method of inspection is fairer, safer, cheaper, and speedier than any other.

Cleinias: That is certainly true.

Athenian: Going forward, then, we can say that politics is the art of knowing how to discover and manage the natures and habits of men's souls.

Cleinias: Exactly so.

652a-653a: Right Education

Athenian: Thus far, the argument implies that well-ordered drinking and intoxication provides benefits and advantages other than insight into human nature. We have to attentively consider this, or we may be entangled in error regarding how and in what way the benefits can be attained.

Cleinias: Proceed.

Athenian: Our doctrine is that right education depends on regulating convivial intercourse.

Cleinias: That is a strong statement!

653a-653c: First Perceptions

Athenian: I maintain that a child's first perceptions of pleasure and pain are a form of virtue and vice.[26] As to wisdom and true and fixed opinions, the man who acquires them is happy even in his declining years. We

---

[26] "I try to understand the idiosyncrasy from which the Socratic equation: Reason = Virtue = Happiness, could have arisen: the weirdest equation ever seen, and one which was essentially opposed to all the instincts of the older Hellenes." The Problem of Socrates - Twilight of the Idols

may say that he who possesses and is blessed by them is a perfect man.[27]

By education, I mean having children acquire suitable habits through training so that they undergo pleasure, friendship, pain, and hatred to rightly implant the first instincts of virtue in souls not yet able to understand their own nature. After attaining reason, they will be in harmony. Taken as a whole, this harmony of the soul is virtue.[28] From the beginning of life to its end, we may define the word education as: Training in pleasure and pain so that a person always ends by hating what he ought to hate, and loving what he ought to love.

Cleinias: Stranger, I think that you are right in all that you have said and are saying about education.

653c-654a: Apollo and the Muses

Athenian: I am glad to hear that you agree with me. Indeed, when rightly ordered, human life corrupts the principle of education by relaxing the discipline of

---

[27] Wisdom, true and fixed opinions = happiness
[28]

pleasure and pain. Pitying the toils our race is born to undergo, the Gods allow men to alternate rest with labor through holy festivals and revelry companions - Apollo, who leads the Muses, and Dionysus. These festivals celebrating the Gods improve men's education.[2930] I wonder if you believe a common saying? Men say all young creatures have loud bodies or voices that always want to move and cry out. Some leap, skip, and overflow with sportiveness and delight, while others utter all sorts of cries. However, animals don't perceive order or disorder in movements, what we call rhythm or harmony.[31] Apollo and the Muses have given men the pleasurable sense of harmony and rhythm, and were appointed by the gods to be our companions in the dance. They stir us to life, and we follow them while joining hands in dances and songs called choruses, a

---

[29] Jowett - And the Gods, pitying the toils which our race is born to undergo, have appointed holy festivals, wherein men alternate rest with labour; and have given them the Muses and Apollo, the leader of the Muses, and Dionysus, to be companions in their revels, that they may improve their education by taking part in the festivals of the Gods, and with their help.

[30] Alternative translation - so the gods, in pity for the human race thus born to misery, have ordained the feasts of thanksgiving as periods of respite from their troubles; and they have granted them as companions in their feasts the Muses and Apollo the master of music, and Dionysus, that they may at least set right again their modes of discipline by associating in their feasts with gods. Discuss Niezsche

[31] This is what distinguishes us from animals

term naturally expressive of cheerfulness.[32] Shall we begin by acknowledging that Apollo and the Muses gave us education?[33] What do you say?

Cleinas: I assent.

654b-654b: The Educated Man

Athenian: Do you agree that the uneducated man hasn't been trained in the chorus while the educated man has been well trained?

Cleinias: Certainly.

Athenian: You agree that the chorus has both dance and song?

Cleinias: True.

Athenian: Then, the man who is well educated will be able to sing and dance properly?

Cleinias: I suppose that he will.

Athenian: Now, what are we saying?

Cleinias: What?

---

[32] Here χορός (dance) is fancifully derived from χατά, "joy." Bury
[33] Apollo and the Muses comes first. This education controls.

654c-654d: Two Kinds of Education

Athenian: The man who is educated sings well and dances well. Shouldn't we add that he sings what is good and dances what is good?

Cleinias: Let us make the addition.

Athenian: We suppose he knows the good to be good, and the bad to be bad, and makes use of them accordingly. Who is better trained in dance and song? Is it the man who doesn't hate evil or delight in good but moves his body and uses his voice in what is understood to be the right manner? Or, is it the man who correctly senses pleasure and pain, welcomes the good, and is offended at evil but he doesn't use his body and voice correctly?

Cleinias: Stranger, there is a great difference in the two kinds of education.

654d-655b: Music

Athenian: If the three of us[34] know what is good in song and dance, then we will also know who is and isn't

---

[34] Megillus isn't in this book even though he is referenced

rightly educated. Otherwise, we won't know where or if education has any safeguards.[35]

Cleinias: True.

Athenian: Like hounds, let's pursue the scent of beautiful figures, melodies, songs, and dances. For, if these escape us, there isn't any use in talking about a rightly educated Hellene or barbarian.

Cleinias: Yes.

Athenian: And what is a beautiful figure or melody? When a manly soul and a cowardly soul have similar troubles, do they use the same figures and gestures? Do they utter the same sounds?

Cleinias: How can they, when the very colors of their faces differ?

Athenian: Good, my friend.   However, I may observe in passing that music has figures and melodies, and is concerned with harmony and rhythm. It is correct to speak of a melody or figure having a good

---

[35] Both Jowett and Bury use 'safeguard.' In Greek, a φυλακτηριον or phylakteirion, 'guard station', but more literally 'a guardian-observation post'. The second half of the word, that is, τηριον, means 'to watch' or 'observe', and emphasizes the need for surveillance. This was used in Republic.

rhythm or harmony. However, we aren't allowed to speak as though we are masters of choruses and describe melody or figure using metaphors such as 'color.' The melodies or figures of the brave or cowardly can only be praised or censured. Not to be tedious, but let's say that without exception figures and melodies are good if they express a virtuous soul or body, or image of the virtuous. Those that express vice are the reverse of good.

Cleinias: Your suggestion is excellent; and let us answer that these things are so.

655b-656b: Fall of Music and Dance

Athenian: Once more, does each person become equally delighted with every sort of dance?

Cleinias: By far, they don't.

Athenian: Then, what leads us astray from the beautiful and good? Don't we all see the same beautiful things? Or, is everything the same and we have opinions of beauty? No one will admit that forms of vice in the dance are more beautiful than forms of virtue. When a man sees that others have a muse with a virtuous character, he doesn't find delight in forms of vice. And yet most people say that excellent music gives pleasure to our souls. This is intolerable and blasphemous. However, there is a much more plausible account of the delusion.

Cleinias: What?

Athenian: Art was forced to adapt to fit men's characters. Choric movements imitate manners occurring in particular actions, fortunes, and dispositions. The words, songs, or dances are suited to men who by nature, habit, or both can't help but feel their pleasure, applaud them, and call them beautiful. But those whose natures, ways, or habits are unsuited cannot delight in or applaud them. They will call them base. There are others whose natures are right but whose habits are wrong, or whose habits are right but whose natures are wrong. They praise one thing, but are pleased at another. They say that all imitations are pleasant, but not good. They are ashamed of dancing and singing in the baser manner while in the presence of those whom they think wise, or of deliberately lending any countenance to such proceedings. However, they secretly find them pleasing.

Cleinias: Very true.

656b-656b: Vicious Dances and Songs

Athenian: Is any harm done to the man who loves vicious dances or songs? How about good done to the man who approves of the opposite sort of pleasure?

Cleinias: I think that there is.

Athenian: To say 'think' is not the word. I would rather you say, 'I am certain.'[36] This is because vicious dances or songs affect a man just as much as associating with, liking, and approving of bad characters. This type of man censures playfully. He suspects that he's bad, and is ashamed to praise his pleasure because it makes him similar to the man who's openly taking pleasure. Can any destiny ever make us undergo a greater good or evil?

---

[36] Plato and the slavery of virtue

Cleinias: I know of none.

656c-657c: Egyptian Laws and Music

Athenian: If a city, or the future, has good laws, they should include musical instruction and amusement.[37] We shouldn't allow poets to teach dances to rhythms, melodies, or words simply because they like them. This isn't how well-conditioned parents will teach their young.[38] Do you think the poet should train his choruses as he pleases, without referencing virtue or vice?

Cleinias: That's quite unreasonable, and we shouldn't think of this.

Athenian: And yet, a man may do this in almost every state. With the exception of Egypt.[39]

Cleinias: And what are Egypt's laws about music and dancing?

---

[37] Time - Now where laws are, or will be in the future,

[38] 'law-abiding'

[39] "Humanity has had to pay dearly for this Athenian having gone to school among the Egyptians (—or among the Jews in Egypt?...) In the great fatality of Christianity, Plato is that double-faced fascination called the "ideal," which made it possible for the more noble natures of antiquity to misunderstand themselves and to tread the bridge which led to the "cross."" Things I Owe the Ancients

Athenian: You will wonder when I tell you. Long ago, it appears they recognized that young citizens had to become habituated to the very principle of which we are now speaking: virtue's forms and strains. They fixed these principles, and exhibited them in patterns in their temples and declared that no painter or artist was allowed to innovate, leave out traditional forms, or invent new ones. To this day, they don't allow arts or music to be altered, and you'll find that their painted or molded works of art have been in the same forms for ten thousand years. This is literally true and not an exaggeration. Their ancient paintings and sculptures are not a whit better, or worse, than those of today. They are made with just the same skill.

Cleinias: How extraordinary!

Athenian: I would rather you say, 'How statesmanlike, how worthy of a legislator!'[40] I know that Egypt has other things which aren't so good, but what I am telling you about music is true and deserves

---

[40] Statesmen - Say rather, worthy in the highest degree of a statesman and a legislator.

consideration, and shows that a lawgiver can, without fear of failure, institute melodies which have a correct and natural truth.[41] However, this must be the work of God, or a divine person.[42] The Egyptian tradition is that the preserved ancient chants were composed by the Goddess Isis. As I said, if a person can find the natural melodies, he may confidently embody them in a fixed and legal form. A love of novelty corrupts men, they grow weary of the old, gain pleasure in the new, and argue that consecrated songs and dances have become antiquated. At any rate, Egypt is far from being corrupted.

Cleinias: Your arguments seem to prove your point.

657c-657d: True Use of Music

Athenian: In the truest sense, can't we confidently say that we use music and choral festivities to rejoice

_____

[41] Isn't this a troubling statement - if there are bad things maybe this understanding of music causes them and can't be separated
[42] divinity

when we think we prosper, and to think we prosper when we rejoice?

Cleinias: Exactly.

Athenian: We aren't able to be still while rejoicing in our good fortune.

Cleinias: True.

Athenian: Our young men break forth into dance and song. We, their elders, deem that we have lost our agility and are fulfilling our part in life by looking at them. We delight in their sports and merry-making and, because we love to think of our former selves, we gladly institute contests for those who are able to awaken in us the memory of our youth.

Cleinias: Very true.

657d-658c: The Festival's Proclamation

Athenian: Without any meaning, the common people say the festival's wisest man is the one who gives us the greatest amount of pleasure and mirth. With mirth being the order of the day, the most honored man, the man who wins the palm, should give the most mirth to the greatest number. Is this a true way of speaking or acting?

Cleinias: Possibly.

Athenian: My dear friend, let's not form a judgment hastily. Let's distinguish between a festival with the citizens assembled, prizes offered, and all sorts of entertainments - gymnastic, musical, and equestrian - where the following proclamation is made: Anyone may enter, and the man who bears the palm will give the spectators the most pleasure. However, without providing definitions, the man who gives pleasure will be crowned the victor, and called the most pleasant. What is likely to be the proclamation's result?

Cleinias: In what respect?

Athenian: There would be various exhibitions. One man would exhibit a rhapsody, like Homer, and another would perform on the lute. Another will have a tragedy, and another a comedy. It wouldn't be astonishing if someone imagined he could gain the prize by exhibiting a puppet-show.[43]   Suppose these competitors and innumerable others meet. Who ought to be the victor?

Cleinias: I do not see how anyone can answer, or even pretend to answer, unless he's heard with his own ears the several competitors. The question is absurd.

658c-658e: Answering the Absurd Question

Athenian: If neither of you can answer who will win the festival, shall I answer the question you call absurd?[44]

Cleinias: By all means.

Athenian: If very small children are to determine the question, they will decide for the puppet show.[45]

Cleinias: Of course.

Athenian: The older children will advocate comedy. Educated women, young men, and people in general will favor tragedy.

Cleinias: Very likely.

_____

[43]

[44] Megillus has been completely absent

[45]

Athenian: I believe that we old men would have the greatest pleasure in hearing, and giving the award to, a rhapsodist who recites the Iliad, Odyssey, or a Hesiodic poem. But, the question is: Who would really be the victor?

Cleinias: Yes.

Athenian: Clearly, we will declare that old men ought to select the victors because our ways are far and away better than any that currently exist anywhere in the world.

Cleinias: Certainly.

658e-659c: How Theater Became Ruined

Athenian: Thus far, I agree with the many: Musical excellence is measured by pleasure. However, the fairest music is not random in its effect. It delights the best and the best educated. It especially delights the one man who is pre-eminently virtuous and educated.[46] Therefore, the judges must be men whose characters include wisdom and courage. The true judge must not

---

[46] he one man who excels all others in virtue and education

draw his inspiration from the theater, nor be unnerved by his own incapacity and the clamor of the many.[47] Having used his lips to appeal to the gods to learn the truth, he isn't cowardly, unmanly, or careless in delivering a truthful judgment. He sits in his proper place as the theater's instructor, not as its disciple. He is the enemy of the ancient and common Hellene custom, still prevalent in Italy and Sicily, of pandering to the spectators' pleasure by leaving judgment to a show of hands. This custom has destroyed the poets. They now desire to please their judges' bad taste which results in spectators instructing themselves. This has ruined the theater because the spectators should only see better men so they can have a higher pleasure. Instead, the spectators' actions have caused the opposite result. Shall I tell you the inference to draw from all this?

Cleinias: What?

---

[47]

659c-660a: Education is a Safeguard

Athenian: For the third or fourth time, we have arrived at the inference that youth are directed and constrained by education towards what the law affirms to be right by reason. We have agreed that the eldest have the best and truly right experiences. Therefore, in order to prevent the child's soul from being habituated to joys and sorrows that aren't in accord with the law and those who follow the law, they should obey, rejoice, and have sorrow at the same things as the aged. I say that chants were invented to enchant and designed to implant that harmony of which we speak. The child's mind is incapable of enduring serious training performed during play, what are called plays and songs. When men are sick and ailing in their bodies, their attendants give them both a wholesome diet of pleasant meats and drinks, and an unwholesome diet in disagreeable things.[48] This is done so that they may learn, as they ought, to like the one and dislike the other.

---

[48] medical

Similarly, the true legislator will persuade. If he cannot persuade, then he ought to compel the poet to express by fair and noble words, rhythms, figures, and melodies the music of temperate and brave and in every way good men.

Cleinias: Stranger, do you really imagine that this is how poets currently compose in states? As far as I can observe, except among us and the Lacedaemonians, there are no regulations like those of which you speak. In other places, novel dancing and music are always being introduced, generally not under the authority of any law, but at the instigation of lawless pleasures. These pleasures are so far from being the same as the Egyptian, or even having similar principles, that they aren't the same.

660b-660d: Theoretical Regulations

Athenian: Most true, Cleinias. I daresay that I may have expressed myself obscurely. I am not speaking of some really existing state of things. I am only saying what regulations I would like to have about music. Thus, there occurred a misapprehension on your part. For, although at times necessary, the task of censuring irremediable evils is never pleasant. However, we don't really differ. Let me ask you: Do you consider such institutions to be more prevalent among the Cretans and Lacedaemonians than among the other Hellenes?

Cleinias: Certainly.

Athenian: And if they were extended to the other Hellenes, wouldn't the present state of things be improved?

Cleinias: Greatly. If Lacedaemonian and Cretan customs were extended and prevailed as we just now said.

660d-661d: Principles

Athenian: Let us see whether we understand one another. Don't Cretan and Lacedaemonian principles of education and music compel poets to define as true that all men (whether great, strong, small, weak, rich, or poor) live good, fortunate, and happy lives, so long as they are temperate and just? On the other hand, if an unjust man is wealthier than Cinyras or Midas, he is wretched and lives in misery?[49] As the poet says, and with truth: I sing not, I care not about him who accomplishes all noble things, not having justice. Let the man who 'draws near and stretches out his hand against his enemies be a just man.' However, if he's unjust, I wouldn't have him 'look calmly upon bloody death' nor 'surpass in swiftness the Thracian Boreas.' He should never have anything called good. Regarding the many, they speak of goods that are not really good. They place health first, beauty next, wealth third, and then innumerable others. For example, to have a keen eye, quick ear, and perfect senses. Or, to be a tyrant and do as they like. For the many, happiness is consummated when they acquire, because they believe acquiring will make them immortal. To this, you and I say that the man knows that the best possession is holiness and that all goods, even health, are evil to the unjust.[50] If man is immortal, then it is the greatest of

_____

[49] Tyrtaeus xii. 6; see Bk. i. 629. Cinyras was a fabled king of Cyprus, son of Apollo and priest of Aphrodite. Midas, king of Phrygia, was noted for his wealth.
[50] The slave

evils to live without justice. If a man is mortal, he may become rich in sight, hearing, other physical senses, and be fortunate in everything but live without justice and virtue for a short time only. If I am not mistaken, these are the truths which you persuade or compel your poets to utter to train your youths accompanied by suitable harmony and rhythm. I plainly declare: The unjust are those who make false distinctions between evils and goods, while the just properly distinguish evils and goods. Let me ask again, do we agree?

Cleinias: I think that we partly agree and partly do not.

661d-662a: Unvirtuous

Athenian: You don't believe an immortal man sense of injustice and insolence wouldn't counterbalance his health, wealth, a tyranny which lasts,[51] strength, and courage to make him miserable?

Cleinias: That is quite true.

---

[51] absolute power in perpetuity,

Athenian: Once more: Suppose that he be valiant, strong, handsome, rich, and able to do whatever he likes throughout his whole life. Still, if he's unrighteous and insolent, wouldn't you both agree that, of necessity, he will live basely? You will surely grant so much?

Cleinias: Certainly.

Athenian: And an evil life too?[52]

Cleinias: I am not equally disposed to grant that.

Athenian: You won't accept that he'll live painfully and to his own disadvantage?

Cleinias: How can I possibly say so?

662a-663a: Speaking as an Otherworldly Lawgiver

Athenian: If you ask how, then we are of two minds and may Heaven make us one. To me, dear Cleinias, the truth of what I am saying is as plain as the fact that Crete is an island. If I were a lawgiver, this is how I would try to make the poets and all the citizens speak: First, I would inflict the heaviest penalties on anyone

---

[52] κακῶς ζῆν, "to live badly" may mean either "to live wickedly" or "to live wretchedly": Clinias takes it in this latter sense.

who dares to say that it is possible for any bad man to lead a pleasant life, or that profit and gain are distinct from justice. There are many other matters about which I'd make my citizens speak differently from today's Cretans and Lacedaemonians. Indeed, I may say that from the world in general.

Tell me, by Zeus and Apollo tell me, what would be the answer if I were to ask these same Gods who were your legislators: Isn't the most just life, also the most pleasant life? Or, are there two lives - one that is just and the other pleasant? If they were to reply: There are two. I would then ask, because that would be the right way to pursue the inquiry: Is the man who leads the life considered most just happier, or the man who leads the most pleasant life?

It would be very strange if they replied: Those who lead the life that is most pleasant. I wouldn't like to put those words into the Gods' mouths. However, from the lips of fathers and legislators, they will come with more propriety. Therefore, I will repeat my former questions to one of them.

Suppose he says: The man who leads the most pleasant life is the happiest. To that, I would rejoin: O my father, didn't you want me to live as happily as possible? However, you also told me to live as justly as possible. Now, the man who gives rules, whether he's the legislator or father, will be in a dilemma. In vain, he'll endeavor to be consistent with himself.

Unless I'm mistaken, if he declared that the happiest life is the life that is most just, everyone would ask: What good and noble principles does the law approve, and which are superior to pleasure? That is, can the just man have what is good if it is separate from pleasure? Shall we say: Glory and fame came from the Gods and are good and noble but are unpleasant while infamy is pleasant? Certainly not, sweet legislator. Shouldn't we say: Even though acting this way provides no pleasure, it is good and honorable to act correctly and to do no wrong. And, while doing wrong is pleasant, it is nevertheless evil and base?

Cleinias: Impossible.

663a-663d: Purging Darkness to Exhibit Truth

Athenian: The view which identifies the pleasant and connects the pleasant to the just, good, and noble has an excellent moral and religious tendency. The opposite view creates variance with the legislator's designs and is infamous because no one can be persuaded to do that which gives more pain than pleasure. To prevent distant prospects from making us dizzy in childhood, the legislator will try to purge darkness and exhibit truth.[53] In some way or another, by customs, praises, and words, he will persuade the citizens that the just and the unjust are only shadows because while injustice seems opposed to justice, the unjust and evil man contemplates it pleasantly and

---

[53] i.e. the lawgiver will make justice clear and distinct by bringing citizens close up to it: discipline in just actions will give them a near and true view of it, and correct the wrong impression due to distance.

justice unpleasantly. Obviously, from the just man's point of view they appear to be the very opposite.

Cleinias: True.

Athenian: And does the inferior soul or the better soul have truer judgment?

Cleinias: Surely, the better soul.

Athenian: Then the unjust life must be more base and depraved. However, is it more unpleasant than the just and holy life?

Cleinias: That seems to be implied in the present argument.

663d-664c: The Useful Lie

Athenian: The argument has proven that the lawgiver who's worth anything could not invent a more useful lie to tell the young, if he ventured to do for their own good, that would better effect them doing what is right voluntarily rather than through compulsion.[54]

Cleinias: Stranger, truth is a noble and lasting thing. However, it is hard to persuade men.

---

[54] Nietszche - Bury useful fiction

Athenian: There are innumerable tales that are improbable, yet readily believed. The Sidonian Cadmus story is one.

Cleinias: What is that story?

Athenian: The legislator takes the story of armed men springing up after the sowing of teeth as proof of his ability to persuade young minds of anything they hear.   Afterwards, he only has to reflect and find the belief that will bring the greatest public advantage, and then use all his efforts to make the whole community utter one and the same word in their songs, tales, and discourses all their life long. If you don't agree with me, there is no reason why you shouldn't argue the other side.

Cleinias: I don't see any argument that can fairly be raised by either of us against what you are now saying.

664c-664e: The Gods Sing of the Best and Happiest Life

Athenian: My next suggestion is that our three choruses sing to the children's young and tender souls, their strains reciting all the noble thoughts of which we have already spoken, or are about to speak. The sum of our discourse shall be: The life the Gods deemed happiest is also the best.[55] We shall affirm this to be a most certain truth so that young disciples' minds will be more likely to receive our words before any other.

Cleinias: I agree with what you say.

Athenian: First, sacred choirs of children in their natural order to sing lustily the heaven-taught to the whole city. Second, the young men under the age of thirty will form a choir to call upon the God Paean to testify to the truth of their words, and will pray to him to be gracious to the youth and to turn their hearts.[56]

---

[55] in asserting that one and the same life is declared by the gods to be both most pleasant and most just, we shall not only be saying what is most true, [664c] but we shall also convince those who need convincing more forcibly than we could by any other assertion.

[56] i.e. "the Healer." Cp. the medicinal sense of ἐπᾴδειν, "enchant," in B4 above. Music is to be a medicine of the soul.

Third, the elders (men from thirty to sixty) will also sing. Those who are too old to sing will tell stories as if they were oracles that illustrate the same virtues as if with an oracle's voice.

Cleinias: Stranger, who is in the third choir? I don't clearly understand what you mean to say about them.

Athenian: And yet, almost everything that I have been saying has been said with a view towards them.[57]

Cleinias: Will you try to be a little plainer?

664e-665c: Dionysian Chorus

Athenian: When our discourse began we spoke of the fiery nature of young creatures. At that time, I said that they called out, couldn't keep their limbs or voices quiet, and jumped about in a disorderly manner. This ability to perceive order makes man different from other animals.[58] We defined rhythm as: the order of motion, and defined harmony as: the order of the voice attaining

---

[57] Everything has been building towards the old and Dionysus
[58]

and mingling high and low. Together, rhythm and harmony are defined as: choric songs. Earlier, I said that the Gods, having pity on us, gave us Apollo and the Muses to be our playfellows and leaders in the dance.[59] I dare say, you will remember, Dionysus was the third.

Cleinias: I remember.

Athenian: Now that I have spoken of choirs for Apollo and the Muses, I will speak of the chorus for Dionysus.[60]

Cleinias: How is the Dionysian chorus arranged? It is strange to hear that elders from thirty to sixty would form a chorus that dances in his honor.

Athenian: Very true. Therefore, we must show a good reason for why it's been proposed.

Cleinias: Certainly.

Athenian: Thus, we agree?

Cleinias: About what?

_____

[59] He said they were to educate. Did he say pity?
[60] [654a-663e]

665c-666d: Getting Old Men to Sing

Athenian: Every man, woman, boy, girl, enslaved, and freemen throughout the whole city should never cease changing and varying harmony and chants to charm themselves. Do we agree that singers should receive pleasure from their hymns and people should never be weary of them?[61]

Cleinias: Everyone will agree.

Athenian: Where will we place those who have great influence because of age and intelligence? Where will they have the greatest influence while singing the fairest strains which will do so much good? Shall we foolishly allow the most beautiful and useful singers to leave?

Cleinias: The argument says we cannot.

Athenian: Then how can we carry out our purpose with decorum?

Cleinias: How?

---

[61] Alternative - That it is the duty of every man and child—bond and free, male and female,—and the duty of the whole State, to charm themselves unceasingly with the chants we have described, constantly changing them and securing variety in every way possible, so as to inspire the singers with an insatiable appetite for the hymns and with pleasure therein.

Athenian: When a man advances in years, he is afraid and becomes reluctant to sing. He no longer finds pleasure in his performances. With age, he becomes more discreet and, when compelled to perform, he becomes even more ashamed. Isn't this true?

Cleinias: Certainly.

Athenian: Well, won't he be more ashamed if he has to stand up and sing in the theater to a mixed audience? Moreover, if he's required to sing like the choirs contending for prizes who've been trained under a singing master, won't he feel shame and discomfort and be unwilling to exhibit.

Cleinias: No doubt.

Athenian: Then how can we reassure him and get him to sing? We begin with the following act:[62] Boys should not taste wine until they are eighteen years old. We will tell them that until they begin work, fire must not be poured onto the fire in their body or soul as a precaution against the excitability of youth. After

---

[62] Shall we not pass a law that

eighteen, they may taste wine in moderation up to the age of thirty. However, a young man should abstain from intoxication and excess wine. At forty, after dinner while at a public mess, he may invite not only the other Gods, but Dionysus above all, to the mystery and festivity of the elder men.[63] He may make use of the wine which Dionysus has given men to lighten the sourness of old age so that we may renew our youth and forget our sorrows. So that, like iron melted in fire, the soul's nature may become soft and impressible. In the first place, wouldn't anyone thus mellowed be more ready, and less ashamed, to sing? Mind you, this wouldn't be done before a large audience but before a moderate company of his familiars and without strangers. Wouldn't he be ready to, as we say, chant and enchant?[64]

Cleinias: He'd be far more ready.

Athenian: You don't find it inappropriate to use such a method to persuade the elders to join us in song?

---

[63]

[64] chants and "incantations" (as we have often called them)

Cleinias: Not at all.

666d-667a: The Strain of Song Old Men Sing

Athenian: What strain will they sing? What muse will they hymn? The strain should clearly be suitable.

Cleinias: Certainly.

Athenian: What strain is suitable for heroes? Shall they sing a choric strain?[65]

Cleinias: Stranger, we of Crete and Lacedaemon only know of strains we have learned and been accustomed to sing in our chorus.

Athenian: Yes, your military way of life is modeled after the camp and not a city.[66] You have never acquired the knowledge of the most beautiful kind of song. You have your young men herding and feeding together like young colts. No one takes his own individual colt, drags him against his will while he rages and foams so that he can be away from his fellows, and given a groom so that he may be attended to and privately trained and

---

[65] a song suited for singing by a chorus at a festival or other public occasion.
[66]

rubbed.[67]   In this manner, he'll receive educational qualities that will make him both a good soldier and a good governor of a state and cities.[68] As we said at first, such a young man would be a greater warrior than anyone sung by Tyrtaeus and, in both individuals and states, he'd honor courage as the fourth rather than the first virtue.

667a-667b: Offending Cretans

Cleinias: Stranger, I once more must complain. You continue to depreciate our lawgivers.

Athenian: My good friend, it wasn't intentional. We must follow where the argument leads.   If the choruses or public theaters don't have a beautiful strain of song then I would like to impart this to those who are, as I say, ashamed and want the best.

Cleinias: Certainly.

---

[67] Highly homo erotic
[68] Aren't they both a polis?

667b-667e: Pleasure's Charm

Athenian:[69] When things have an accompanying charm, it's either something which makes it the very best, or something which possesses some rightness or utility. For example: In general, eating, drinking, and using food are accompanied by a charm called pleasure. This is right. Their true and right utility is showing the health of each serving.

Cleinias: Just so.

Athenian: Learning's accompanying charm is pleasure, and its utility is truth and the qualities of right, profitable, good and noble.

Cleinias: Exactly.

Athenian: In the imitative arts, they produce a pleasurable charm when they succeed in making likenesses. Yes?

Cleinias: Yes.

---

[69] The following passage (down to 669 B) deals with the considerations of which a competent judge must take account in the sphere of music and art. He must have regard to three things—"correctness" (the truth of the copy to the original), moral effect or "utility," and "charm" or pleasure. Though this last, by itself, is no criterion of artistic excellence, it is a natural "concomitant" (in the mind of the competent judge) when the work of art in question possesses a high degree of both "utility" and "correctness."

Athenian: However, speaking generally, the imitation's truth or rightness is based on pleasure but on equal proportions of its quality or quantity.[70]

Cleinias: Yes.

Athenian: Then judged by pleasure, which neither makes nor furnishes utility, truth, or likeness, and produces hurtful qualities. When other qualities are absent, imitative arts exist solely for the charm appropriately termed 'pleasure'.[71]

Cleinias: Are you speaking of harmless pleasure?

Athenian: Yes. I define amusement as: Doing neither harm nor good in any degree worth speaking of.

Cleinias: Very true.

667e-669b: The One Standard

Athenian: With our principles we assert: Rather than pleasure or false opinion judging imitations, they should be judged by whether the equal isn't equal or the symmetrical isn't symmetrical. That is, it doesn't matter

---

[70] a "likeness" must be "equal" to its original both in character and size.
[71] Think about from perspective of a slave

if somebody thinks or likes something, they must only be judged by one standard - truthfulness.

Cleinias: Quite true.

Athenian: Is all music regarded as representative and imitative?

Cleinias: Certainly.

Athenian: Thus, we cannot admit a doctrine stating music is to be judged by pleasure. A man shouldn't look to pleasure as the criterion for music because it doesn't have any real excellence. This is because music imitates the good.

Cleinias: Very true.

Athenian: Furthermore, those who seek the best kind of songs and music should only seek the truth and, as we were saying, the truth is that imitation consists of most closely rendering the thing imitated.

Cleinias: Certainly.

Athenian: And everyone will admit that musical compositions are all imitative and representative. Won't poets and spectators and actors all agree on this?

Cleinias: They will.

669b-670b: Music's Peculiarity

Athenian: Can't we say that a man who's a competent judge of any imitated art - whether drawing, music, or any other art - must possess three things: knowledge of the true, knowledge of the imitation, and knowledge of the imitation being well executed?

Cleinias: Certainly.

Athenian: Then let's discuss music's peculiar difficulty. The topic requires the greatest care because it is more celebrated than any other kind of imitation and, if a man makes a mistake in imitating music, he may welcome evil dispositions and injure himself.   In addition, because poets are artists inferior in character to the Muses, who would never err by assigning men's words to women's gestures and songs, the mistake may be difficult to discern.[72]   The Muses would never

---

[72] In what follows, the main features censured are—incongruity, when the words, tunes and gestures of an acted piece of music are out of harmony; senselessness, when tunes and gestures are divorced from words; barbarousness, when the thing represented is paltry or uncouth (such as a duck's quack); virtuosity, when the performer makes a display of the control he has over his limbs and instruments, like a mountebank or "contortionist." All these are marks of bad music from the point of

combine a freeman's melodies and gestures, and include the rhythms of slaves and baser men.[73] Nor would they begin with rhythms and gestures of freemen, and then assign them an opposite character of melody or words. Nor would they mix up, as if they were all one, the voices and sounds of animals, men, instruments, and every other sort of noise.

Human poets are fond of introducing this sort of inconsistent mixture and make themselves ridiculous in the eyes of those who, as Orpheus says, 'are ripe for true pleasure.' Even though the experienced see their confusion, the poets go on separating rhythm and figure of dance from melody. They make havoc by setting words to meter and, while using only a lyre or flute, they separate melody and rhythm from words.[74] Without words, it's difficult to see and recognize how harmony and rhythm imitate a worthy object.[75] Furthermore, we must acknowledge that this sort of thing aims at

---

view of the educationist and statesman, since they are neither "correct" nor morally elevating.

[73]

[74]

[75] Earlier he said we can't see music

swiftness, smoothness, and brutish noise. The flute and lyre are exceedingly coarse and tasteless because they aren't used to accompanying dance and song. Unaccompanied, the use of lyre or flute leads to every sort of irregularity and trickery.

This is all rational enough. However, we are considering how our thirty to fifty year old, and perhaps over fifty years old, choristers are to use the Muses.[76] Thus far, we have considered urging these fifty years' old choristers to train better so they can sing through quick perception and knowledge of harmonies and rhythms. How else will they know to properly sing a melody in the Dorian mode, or another rhythm the poet assigned?

Cleinias: Clearly they won't.

670b-671d: Training Old Men

Athenian: Regarding harmony and rhythm, the many ridiculously imagine that they know what is proper and what isn't. They can sing and step

---

76

rhythmically through force because they don't realize their ignorance. Every melody has a suitable harmony and rhythm which is unsuitable when wrong.

Cleinias: That is most certain.

Athenian: As we were saying: Can a man who doesn't know anything know that the thing is right?

Cleinias: Impossible.

Athenian: It appears we're discovering that the men we've invited to be our newly-appointed choristers are their own masters and were compelled to sing. Therefore, they must be educated to follow rhythmic steps for dance, and notes and harmonies suitable for song, for men their age and character. Their own singing performance can provide innocent pleasure, and lead younger men to dutifully delight in welcoming good dispositions. Having such training, their knowledge will be more accurate than that of the common people, or even the poets. For the poet inevitably knows the laws of melody and rhythm but not the third point - that is, whether the imitation is good or not. The aged chorus must know all three in order to choose the best and that nearest to the best. If not, they won't be able to charm young men's souls in the way of virtue. The argument's original design was intended to eloquently aid the Chorus of Dionysus, and this has been accomplished to the best of our ability. Let's see whether we were right: I should imagine that a drinking assembly is likely to become more and more tumultuous as the drinking goes on. As we were saying at first, this will certainly be the case.

Cleinias: Certainly.

Athenian: When a man's more than naturally high, within his heart he is glad and will say anything without anyone being able to restrain him. He fancies that he is able to rule over himself and all mankind.

Cleinias: Quite true.

Athenian: Weren't we saying that on such occasions a drinker's soul becomes like iron heated in the fire, and grows softer and younger, and is easily molded by someone who knows how to educate and fashion them as if they were young. This fashioner is the same as the man who was in charge during their youthful days: the good legislator.[77] He ought to enact banquet laws for when a man is confident, bold, impudent, and unwilling to wait his turn so that he can have silence, speech, drinking, and music, he will change his character into the opposite. Therefore, such laws will take up arms at the approach of insolence, and infuse him with the just, noble, and divine fear we call: reverence and shame.

Cleinias: True.

671d-672a: Guardians: Regulating Drinking

Athenian: The law's guardians, and their fellow-workers, are the calm and sober generals amidst the drinkers. Without their help, it is more difficult to fight against drink than to fight against an enemy army whose commander isn't calm. The man more than 60 years old is unwilling to obey a Dionysiac feast

---

[77]

commander shall suffer a disgrace as great or greater than the man who disobeys military leaders.

Cleinias: Right.

Athenian: If we regulated drinking and amusement in this way, wouldn't our revelry with companions be improved? Instead of leaving as enemies, the companions would leave as better friends than when they arrived. Wouldn't their whole intercourse be improved if it were regulated and observed by law, and the sober led the drunken?

Cleinias: I think yes, if drinking were regulated as you propose.

672a-672e: Bacchic Furies

Athenian: Let's not simply censure Dionysus' gift as bad and unfit for the state. Wine has many excellences, pre-eminently it helps overcome fear of speaking to the many because they might misconceive and misunderstand what is said.

Cleinias: To what do you refer?

Athenian: According to a tradition, or story, that has somehow crept about the world, Dionysus' stepmother robbed him of his wits and, out of revenge, he inspired the Bacchic furies, dancing madnesses, and gave men wine.[78] I leave traditions concerning the Gods to those who think they may be uttered safely.[79] I only know that, at birth, no animal is mature or perfect in intelligence.[80] In the intermediate period, in which he has not yet acquired his own proper sense, he rages and roars without rhyme or reason. Once he's gotten his legs, he jumps about without rhyme or reason. As you will remember, we've already said this is the origin of music and gymnastics.

Cleinias: To be sure, I remember.

Athenian: Didn't we say that man's sense of harmony and rhythm sprang from man's beginning thanks to Apollo and the Muses, and Dionysus?

Cleinias: Certainly.

---

[78] Wine was given in vengeance? in vengeance therefor he brought in Bacchic rites and all the frenzied choristry, and with the same aim bestowed also the gift of wine.

[79] .e. the "frenzied" motion ascribed to Dionysus is, rather a natural instinct exhibited in all child-life, and D. helps to reduce it to rhythm.

[80]

Athenian: The first story implied that man was given wine out of revenge in order to make him mad. However, our doctrine is that wine was given to him as a balm to implant modesty in the soul, and health and strength in the body.

Cleinias: Stranger, that's precisely what was said.

Athenian: Then half the subject may now be considered to have been discussed. Shall we proceed to the consideration of the other half?

Cleinias: What is the other half, and how do you divide the subject?

672e-673e: Half of the the Whole Choral Art

Athenian: The whole choral art is also in our view the whole of education.[81] Regarding choral art, the parts which have to do with the voice are called rhythms and harmonies .

Cleinias: Yes.

_____

[81]

Athenian: The body and voice move with common rhythm. Gesture is peculiar to the body, while the movement of the voice is called song.

Cleinias: Most true.

Athenian: The voice's sound reaches and educates the soul. This we ventured to term music.

Cleinias: We were right.

Athenian: When an amusement, the movement of the body is termed dancing. However, this may be called gymnastics when extended and pursued to scientifically train the body for excellence.

Cleinias: Exactly.

Athenian: Music was one half of the choral art and has been completely discussed. Shall we proceed to the other half or not? What would you like?

Cleinias: My good friend, when you are talking with a Cretan and Lacedaemonian,[82] and we have discussed music but not gymnastics, there is only one answer either of us is likely to make to such an inquiry.

82

Athenian: While your answer contained a question, I understand what you say as a command to proceed with gymnastics.

Cleinias: You quite understand me. Do as you say.

Athenian: I will. There won't be any difficulty in speaking intelligibly about a subject both of you are more familiar with than with music.

Cleinias: There will not.

Athenian: Should we look for the origin of gymnastics in the tendency which exists in all animals for rapid motion. As we were saying, man has attained the sense of rhythm which allowed him to create and invent dancing to unite arousing melodies and awakening rhythms in the form of the choral art?

Cleinias: Very true.

Athenian: And one part of this subject has been already discussed by us, and there still remains another to be discussed?

Cleinias: Exactly.

673e-674c: Final Word on Drinking

Athenian: I have a final word to add to my discourse about drinking.

Cleinias: What more do you have to say?

Athenian: If a city seriously means to enforce temperance by regulating drinking, the city will use the same principle so that people will gain victory over all pleasures.   However, if a person may drink whenever and with whomever he likes, then the State makes drinking an amusement like any other indulgence.   I would never allow a city or man to practice drinking.   I would go further than the Cretans and Lacedaemonians, and am disposed to the Carthaginian laws which dictate that on a campaign they should only drink water and never be allowed to taste wine.   I would add to this that city slaves, male or female, should never drink wine.   Magistrates shouldn't drink wine during their year in office, nor should pilots of vessels, judges on duty, nor those consulting about any matter of importance.   People should drink in the day-time, unless as a consequence of exercise or as medicine, nor at night when any man or woman is minding children. There are countless other cases in which those with good sense and good laws ought not to drink wine. If what I say is true, no city will need many vineyards, and their husbandry and way of life will follow an appointed order. Cultivation of the vine will be the most limited and least common of their employments. Stranger, if you agree, this shall be the crown of my discourse about wine.

Cleinias: Excellent. We agree.

www.ingramcontent.com/pod-product-compliance
Lightning Source LLC
Chambersburg PA
CBHW082048220626
47052CB00007B/1249